Crispin

The Pig Who Had it All

Ted DeWan

PICTURE CORGI BOOKS

D0452588

This book is dedicated to
Scott,
Chris,
Tim,
and of course,
Crispin,
who helped me put the bits together

CRISPIN, THE PIG WHO HAD IT ALL
A PICTURE CORGI BOOK : 0 552 546275

First published in Great Britain by Doubleday, a division of Transworld Publishers

PRINTING HISTORY
Doubleday edition published 2000
Picture Corgi edition published 2001

1 3 5 7 9 10 8 6 4 2

Copyright © Ted Dewan, 2000

Designed by Ian Butterworth

The right of Ted Dewan to be identified as the author and illustrator of this work has
been asserted in accordance with the Copyright, Designs and Patents Act 1988

Picture Corgi Books are published by Transworld Publishers,
61-63 Uxbridge Road, London W5 5SA,
a division of The Random House Group Ltd,
in Australia by Random House Australia (Pty) Ltd,
20 Alfred Street, Milsons Point, Sydney, NSW 2061,
in New Zealand by Random House New Zealand Ltd,
18 Poland Road, Glenfield, Auckland 10,
and in South Africa by Random House (Pty) Ltd,
Endulini, 5A Jubilee Road, Parktown 2193

Printed in Singapore

www.booksattransworld.co.uk
www.wormworks.com

PLEASE NOTE THAT THE CRISPIN IN THIS BOOK IN NO WAY RESEMBLES ANY ACTUAL CRISPINS, LIVING OR DEAD

Crispin Tamworth was a pig who had it all.

And at Christmas, he got even more.

One Christmas, he got a  Zybox™ Teddy-bot.

But by Easter,
    he was bored with it...

...and then it got broken.

The next Christmas, he got a
SPEEDPONY™ SHOCKJOCKEY.

But by Valentine's day,
          he was bored with it...

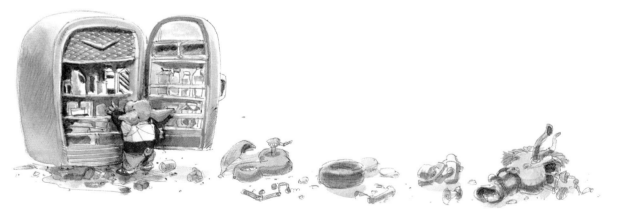

...and then it got broken.

Last Christmas, he got a GIGA-PIGSTATION™ and all the latest computer games.

But by New Year's Day, he was already bored with it...

...and, as usual,  it got broken.

This Christmas, when he woke up early
to peek at his toys,
Crispin found an enormous box.

Master
Crispin,
In this box,
you will find
the only thing
you do not have.
It's the very best
thing in the
whole wide world
S

"Oh boy!"
squeaked Crispin.

He pulled the ribbon,
lifted the top of the box,
and peeped inside.

But the box
was empty.

There was nothing inside at all.

Crispin sat by the Christmas tree and cried.

"What's the matter, Crispin dear?" cooed Mrs Tamworth.

"Santa gave me nothing for Christmas," snuffled Crispin.

"Weren't you a good pig this year?" grunted Mr Tamworth.

"Oh, it must have been a mistake," said Mrs Peck, the housekeeper. "I'm sure Santa didn't mean to make you sad."

But Crispin
was very sad.

He shoved the box
out of the front door.

Then he went
to his room and
stayed there all
Christmas morning.

He didn't even
come down
for his Christmas
dinner.

Crispin sat by his window
and watched as a rabbit and a raccoon
walked into his front yard.

"What a great box!"
said the rabbit.
"Come on, let's take it,"
said the raccoon.

But Crispin didn't want anyone else to take his box.

"Hm, this is no fun," he said.

Soon Crispin was cold. So he went back inside.

The next day, Nick and Penny
crept back to play in Crispin's box.

"Hey, that's MINE," Crispin oinked. "Get out!"
"We're not wrecking anything," said Penny.
"We're playing Space Base."

"I don't see any Space Base," grunted Crispin.
"Look out, Penny!" screamed Nick. "ALIEN!"

"I'm not the alien, YOU'RE the alien," said Crispin.
"This is my property – now you GET OUT!"

"BZZZAP!" shouted Nick. "GOTCHA, ALIEN SCUM!"

"Ha! Missed me by a mile," squealed Crispin.

And so they
all played
Space Base
until sunset.

On Saturday,
Mr Tamworth gave
Crispin his pocket money.

"Aren't you going off to the
arcade today?" asked
Mr Tamworth.

"Not today,"
said Crispin.

"Nick and Penny might come by."

Nick and Penny did come by, and they all played **STORE**,

PIRATES,

CASTLE,

and, of course,
their favourite...

SPACE BASE.

They played so long that Crispin was late for supper.

That night,
the weather changed.
It rained and rained.
All the snow melted.

So did
Crispin's box.

"My box is ruined,"
Crispin sobbed.
"Now my friends won't
come over any more."

But, of course, his friends did come over.

"Look at all this stuff!" shouted Nick.
  "Aw, it's all broken," said Crispin. "It's junk."

But his friends didn't think so.

They helped Crispin
gather the broken bits
of the ZYBOX™ TEDDY-BOT

and the
SPEEDPONY™
SHOCKJOCKEY

and the
GIGA-PIGSTATION™

and they all had
a hopping good
game of...

They played until way after supper time,
and almost missed dessert.

One Friday after school,
Crispin brought his friends back to play.

"Hi, kids!" said Mrs Peck. "Come in and
see our brand new fridge. It's just arrived,
and it makes
ice-cream!"

"Brilliant!" piped
Crispin's friends.

"Oh, Crispin," said Mrs Peck, "the fridge delivery man took away all that junk in your room. Now it's nice and tidy."

"JUNK!" shouted Crispin. "That wasn't junk!

It was a store... and a pirate ship... and a castle... and SPACE BASE... and you threw it all away!"

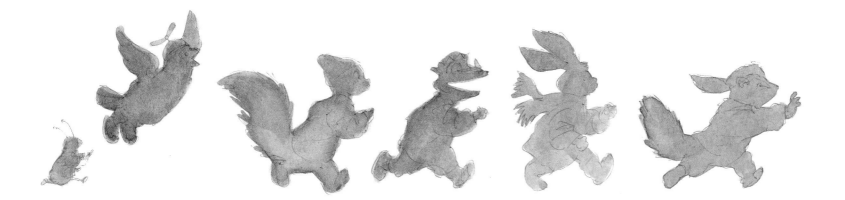

"All my pals will go away.
There's nothing here to play with."

Crispin wept.

But right there in his own back garden
was the great big box
that the fridge came in.

Crispin went
and peeped inside
the empty box...

...and he saw
that it was full.